DATING THE Doubter

KARLA DOYLE

www.karladoyle.com

Series concept by Kameron Claire.

Edited by Grace Bradley Editing

DATING THE DOUBTER © Karla Doyle, 2022

This Valentine's Day, our heroes and heroines are skipping the dating apps to attend one of MatchMakers' famous speed-dating events. Is five minutes enough to feel a spark of chemistry? Can love truly be in the air?

Go on a speed date with us and find out!

MatchMakers Valentine's Day Speed-Dating Event

Are you single and seeking a special love connection? Why not consider a social event in a friendly and relaxed environment where you'll meet twelve available, local singles via a series of five-minute mini-dates?

Don't waste days or weeks (or more!) looking at profile pictures, reading bios, and chatting idly online, only to meet in-person and find you have no connection. Swallow your fears and come to our event with likeminded individuals hoping to meet that special someone.

Love connections are our specialty at MatchMakers! It's fun, easy, and conducted in a relaxed, pressure-free environment.

A MatchMakers professional will contact you with additional information, including a pre-registration questionnaire, and sample questions for our speed-dating events.

We can't wait to share a fun-filled evening with you!

chapter
one

HARRISON

Happy Valentine's Day, Matchmakers!

THE GLOSSY BANNER taunts me as I walk into the hotel's private banquet hall. As if acknowledging "the most romantic day of the year" isn't enough, I'm about to spend it with not one, but two-dozen true-love believers. All because I have a head for financial figures instead of the gift of geek. Fuck my life.

Not really. Outside of tonight's unfortunate turn of events, my life's pretty great. How many thirty-three-year-olds can say they co-own one of the hottest online games on the market? Two, that's how many. And I'm one of them.

Normally, I'm glad to be the partner with a head for numbers. My buddy Greg is the tech half of our brainchild, and I've never needed—or wanted—to understand his geeky gifts. He makes the games do the fun stuff. I turn the fun stuff into green stuff. It works really damn well.

For the first time, I'm wishing our roles were reversed. If I were the programmer, I'd be at the office right now. Fixing whatever it is that needs to be fixed to get Odyssey of Onixath up and running. I have no idea what that's going to entail. When Greg and his team start talking, it might as well be a foreign language.

Bottom line—the game stopped working.

You think malls are crazy busy on Black Friday? That's nothing compared to the onslaught of calls, social media messages, and emails flooding our support center. Players don't like dying in-game, but they really lose it when faced with the black screen of death. We're talking angry-mob-with-pitchforks level shit.

Best to step aside and let the geek squad work their magic. Still, I *should* be holed up in my twentieth-floor corner office, monitoring subscriptions and merchandise transactions. I could be putting together offers that'll soothe our temporarily game-deprived customers' tempers while also putting more money in the company coffers. But that's not where I am.

I'm at a fucking speed-dating event. On fucking Valentine's Day. Because my business partner isn't only a computer and gaming genius, he's a hopeless romantic. And I do mean hopeless. I've tried getting him to see the glaring truth—love is like a drug. It lures you in, gives you a temporary high. But endorphins don't last. There's always a crash.

Greg has met "the one" more times than I can count, and that's saying something, since I'm a numbers guy. He falls fast and hard, every time. Then comes the real fall, when his "soulmate" inevitably either dumps him, or shows her true colors. Either way, it always ends. Then begins again with the next woman he meets at one of these speed-dating gigs. For a genius, he's not very bright.

If I were truly a good friend, I'd turn around and walk away, instead of taking his place at tonight's "desperates anonymous" meetup. A last-minute no-show would throw off the male-to-female ratio, thereby pissing off the organizer, who'd ban him from future events. That's what he claimed when he begged me to cover for him. Literally begged. It would've been funny if he wasn't serious. I'm going to have to go through with this.

"Shit." My muttered curse draws the attention of a nearby redhead.

Apparently, profanity and a scowl are a beacon, because she's smiling in my face within seconds. "Hi, I'm Vanessa. Obviously." She taps the nametag stuck to a body-hugging green dress. "You're new."

"Actually, I'm Harrison."

"You're so funny!"

I try not to grimace at her laugh, but it's shrill enough to shatter glass. Definitely won't be passing Vanessa's name along to Greg. I need my partner's eardrums intact.

"Let's get you signed in." She links her arm with mine. "Not that I want to share you with anyone."

Holy shit. The game's already afoot.

"Think I'd better sign in on my own," I say, disentangling from the woman clinging to me like a staticky sweater. "Don't want it to seem like I've already found my match before the event has started." I give her a wink. Just because it's bullshit doesn't mean I can't play along like a pro. "I'll see you later."

"Can't wait." She waves while walking toward the bar.

The bar where they're serving cocktails to a handful of attendees. Excellent. That'll be my next stop.

I scope out the room on my way to the clearly marked check-in table. A quick head count tells me I'm the last to arrive. Everyone's dressed on the formal side, as per the rules. Too bad I couldn't have seen Greg in action here. I've known the guy since high school, and he's not a dress-to-impress kind of guy. I honestly didn't think he owned a suit.

I, on the other hand, own a closetful. The fact that I was already wearing one made it easier for Greg to call me out as his replacement. Nobody else in the office was positioned to step in. Maybe I'll start wearing jeans to work —after I buy a pair.

There's nobody manning the station when I reach the table, and no "Hi, my name is" sticker to grab. It's a sign to get the hell out of here. I can say I tried, right?

Wrong. "Fuck," I say, dragging a hand over my face.

"We suggest limiting profanity use during the event. It gives the wrong impression."

"Or an honest one," I say, turning toward the female voice that's equal parts soft and assertive. My favorite kind. I've got my charming-asshole smile in place when our gazes meet, and the owner of the sexy voice clearly isn't impressed. Which is too bad, because she's gorgeous. As in ticks-every-box—and a few I didn't realize I had —gorgeous.

"You must be Harrison Bernard." Her fire-engine-red lips remain poker straight. "It's unfortunate Greg couldn't make it tonight. He's a great guy. He's always a welcome addition to our events."

Ouch. There's no mistaking that subtle insult. The lady has claws. Finely pointed claws.

"Trust me, nobody wishes he were here more than I do. Except maybe Greg. He's a sucker for these matchmaker things."

Her amber, almond-shaped eyes narrow. "If Greg hadn't called me with his personal guarantee that you'd pass the vetting process, you'd be out the door right now, Mr. Bernard. You may find 'these matchmaker things' off-putting, but it's Greg's reputation on the line if you take your unfounded negative bias to the table. I hope you'll keep that in mind, for your friend's sake, and out of respect for the attendees who've been looking forward to tonight's opportunity to connect with someone special."

Berated by a salesperson pushing the biggest crock of crap around. I don't think so. "I know what women want to hear. There'll be plenty of smiling faces at the lonely-hearts club tonight."

"I bet *yours* is the loneliest heart in the room." She doesn't look up from writing my name on a sticker in the angriest all-caps I've ever seen. "And that you've earned it."

"I'll take that bet."

Her head jerks up, fury swirling in her pretty eyes. "Excuse me?"

"I said, I'll take that bet." I relieve her of the Sharpie she's holding, cap it and set it aside, then collect my nametag and affix it to my suit jacket, calmly smoothing it while holding her fiery gaze. "After I've played nice at your event tonight, I'm taking *you* on a date. A real one, not a group project."

"I'm not going out with you."

"I'm sure it's against company policy, but I won't be a MatchMakers member after tonight. You won't get in trouble with your boss."

"I *am* the boss. I own this franchise."

Not going to lie, I'm kind of turned on by that information. Also by the contempt in her voice. I'm anti-love, not anti-passion.

"I wouldn't go out with you if you were the last available man alive. I'd let the human race die out before I'd get involved with a man like you." She's beautiful, sexy, well-spoken, business-minded, snarky, and she loathes me.

Fuck me, I might be in love after all.

EDEN

The absolute nerve of this guy. Insulting my business. Assuming it couldn't even *be* my business. Having the balls to *inform* me we're going on a date—a date for the sole purpose of proving me wrong. I've never met a cockier bastard, and boy, have I met a lot.

I'd have kicked his arrogant ass to the curb if it wouldn't mess up the flow of the speed-dating. My guests have been looking forward to this Valentine's Day event for months. The women are intelligent. They'll see through his smarmy façade, see him for the crass asshole he truly is. Even if they don't, I'll make sure none of them take things further. Anyone who submits Harrison's name as a potential match will get vetoed. He might've waltzed through the door, but he's not getting past the gatekeeper.

"The bar is open during the mingling portion of the evening. Your drinks are included in the event fee, and there's a two-cocktail limit to ensure sobriety. I assume Greg told you we have a zero-tolerance policy for impairment from any source." Because I can't resist, I add, "Your emotional impairment excluded, of course."

Most men would fume at being insulted to their face. Not this one. He laughs so loud, it turns every head in our direction. Then he smiles. An entirely different smile from that slick, bullshit version from a few minutes ago. This smile is wide, genuine, and reaches his eyes, which I hate myself for noticing are a lovely shade of bluish green. He's a very attractive man when he's not trying to be.

"I promise to be on my best behavior, Miss...?"

"Ms. Greene." I correct the salutation strictly to take control. Mentally acknowledging his good looks is bad enough, I can't have any hint of it escaping my guard. "Enjoy your evening, Mr. Bernard. I hope you're lucky enough to find the love match you weren't expecting."

The witty retort I'm anticipating doesn't materialize. Just a continuation of the smile that causes a foolish and unwelcome whirling low in my belly.

I'm blaming the sushi I picked up from a food truck earlier. There's no way I'm attracted to a man like Harrison Bernard. I can't be.

chapter
two

EDEN

I'D LIKE to say I haven't noticed Harrison's popularity with tonight's match-seekers, but I'm not a liar. I've noticed. Even if I were blind, I'd still have noticed, because I would have smelled the damn pheromones in the air.

The man is like freaking catnip. And it's not just the women gravitating toward him, though every single one of them has done the human equivalent of rubbing against his leg. The men are drawn to him, too. A couple of them engaged him in brief business conversation. He shared some sports talk with a former semi-pro hockey player. And two of the men who checked the "interested in women only" box on their questionnaire have clearly realized they have bisexual leanings.

I have no idea which box Harrison would have checked, had he completed the intake form, but my gut says he's just being polite to the two lingering males. Or maybe it's not my gut, it's my long-neglected vagina. It definitely wants Harrison to be on the vaginas-only team.

Ugh, I do not want to be attracted to Harrison Bernard. Do. Not. Want.

It's fine. I can appreciate his appeal from a safe distance for a few hours. He'll blow out of my life permanently once the event is wrapped up.

Wrapped up. Like his cock would be if I had sex with him...

Bad brain, bad. I'm never having sex with Harrison Bernard, no matter how hot it would be. An assumption I'm making because every woman in the room—and at least two of the guys—want to jump his bones. Anthropologically speaking, that's proof of virility, right?

Harrison's potential potency is irrelevant. Getting him out of my business and my life is all that matters. Might as well hurry that along a little.

I ring the bell to get everyone's attention, Harrison's included, though I pointedly avoid meeting his gaze as I address the group. "Thank you all for attending the MatchMakers Valentine's Day event. I know you're as excited as I am."

"More!" someone calls, drawing a laugh from everyone in the room.

"During our speed-dating round, ladies will stay seated and gentleman will move from table to table when the bell sounds. My assistants will be keeping a respectful yet watchful eye. If you need anything, simply raise your hand. We'll take a short break after the first six dates. If the ladies would now find their designated tables, and the gentlemen would pick up their labeled folders from the ledge by the window, we'll review how to use the scoring cards, then get the speed-dating round underway."

There's a hum in the air as they get sorted, but it's not the voices. It's energy. Excitement. Seeing the happily-everafters that result from these MatchMakers events never gets old. But it's this moment, the hopeful anticipation that maybe tonight, a soulmate will be found…this is my favorite part of the job.

Once everyone's ready, I give them a few sample questions from the MatchMakers program, instruct them how to use the cards, and tell them to have fun. Only then do I meet Harrison's gaze.

He's smiling, and it's definitely at me. The attendee folder is tucked under one arm, and I bet he hasn't even opened it.

No. No betting. Not with this man. He's clearly a man who expects to win, and I'm not going to be his prize. Not in any manner. Yet I can't seem to summon irritation that he's not following along with my how-to speech. Part of me likes that he's not taking the event seriously, that he's not interested in making a love connection with the women at their respective tables.

That part of me needs a slap. I stopped falling for men like Harrison a long time ago, and I'm not about to have a relapse.

"Okay," I say, forcing my eyes from the slice of *GQ* perfection named Harrison Bernard. Hovering my hand over the timer button, I smile at my guests, and say, "Is five minutes enough time to feel a spark of chemistry? Could your true love be in this room tonight? Let's find out!"

Time to focus on the people truly interested in being at the event, not the man my body is interested in getting better acquainted with.

EDEN

"I assume these are blank." I wave the folder of scorecards Harrison hands me.

"You know they're not. You watched me writing on them."

"I wasn't watching *you* do anything. I watch the room, as the host." The first statement is a fib, but I'll never confess it.

"All right." It's acquiescence, but the twinkle in his eyes says he doesn't believe me. "Aren't you going to look?" he asks, when I set his folder on the table, unopened.

I shake my head. "To protect everyone's privacy, I review the matches in my office."

"I don't need protecting." He nods at his folder. "Take a look."

"Why? So I can see whatever insulting comments you made about the lovely women you were fortunate enough to talk with tonight? Or were you doodling boobs and dicks, and you want to see if I'll blush?"

The space between his dark eyebrows narrows, and the twinkle beneath them dims. "I'm not a total asshole. Or a thirteen-year-old."

It's a trap. A big hunk of stinky cheese and I'm not interested in being the mouse. Guilt gets the best of me, though, along with curiosity. "Fine, I'll look." Sighing, I pick up the folder. I don't want to see who he chose as a match. I shouldn't care who caught his interest, but the knot twisting in my stomach is proof that I do. The sooner I look at his damn scorecards, the sooner I can get him out of my life, and reset my attraction meter to someone more appropriate.

Hands in his pants pockets—which is entirely too sexy

a look on him—he watches me open the folder. I don't give him the satisfaction of looking up, but I swear I can *feel* him smiling as I flip through the pages. Each page is marked as a match, with each of the twelve women's names crossed out, and *Ms. Greene* written in their places.

"This is ridiculous." I close the folder with a slap, then toss it on the table. "You can't match with me. You know nothing about me."

"Enough to know I want to know more."

There's a traitorous flutter in my chest, but I tamp it down. "And I know enough to know I know enough."

There's a moment with both of us replaying my convoluted comeback, then another with our shared laughing. Which feels good. Better than I'd like it to.

"Thank you for filling in for Greg tonight." I turn my attention to packing supplies into a pink case. "I'm sure he appreciated it and so do I."

"You're welcome. I enjoyed it, actually." When I don't bite, he moves closer, picking up a stack of papers and lightly tapping to align the edges, then handing them to me —but not letting go. "I enjoyed meeting you."

"I...didn't hate meeting you."

"It's a start. Go out with me. Maybe you won't hate having dinner with me, either." Oh, he's good. As slick and charming as they get. So full of it, it seems natural. Those are the worst kind.

"I'm sure I wouldn't hate it." I tug the papers from his manicured hand, and continue gathering my things. "You're Greg's business partner, so you're obviously doing well. Being a semi-bigshot, you probably have connections. You'd take me somewhere exclusive, with menus that don't have prices for their expensive wine which we'll drink in our private, corner booth. You'll listen to me talk, enough to make me feel important—occasionally peppering the conversation with details about you intended to impress and seduce me. Then we'll go to your fancy condo on some ridiculously high floor, have mind-blowing sex, and I'll never hear from you again."

"That's detailed, Ms. Greene. Is that what you were thinking about while you weren't watching me?" His smile would dazzle a less-savvy woman.

The best he's getting from me is an eyeroll.

"Your fantasy got a few things wrong, though," he says, moving close enough that I get a hint of aftershave.

"The part about the mind-blowing sex? That's unfortunate. I was giving you the benefit of the doubt, but —" I lower my gaze to the front of his pants, then shake my head. "I guess success and money can't fix everything."

His laugh is deep and rich, sending a ripple of *yes please* straight between my legs. "I don't want to take you out anymore, I *need* to. One date. Say yes, Eden."

Our faces are way too close together when I jerk my head up. Dammit, I've given him what he wants, I've let him surprise me. A temporary mistake. "Am I supposed to swoon because you used my first name?"

He shakes his head. "I used it because it's beautiful, like you."

"Ah, so *this* is where I'm supposed to swoon. Sorry, it's not happening. I know your type and I don't fall for it." *Anymore.*

"Forget falling, I don't want that. I want you to join me for a nice dinner, interesting conversation, and if you want, a night of that mind-blowing sex you fantasized about." His wink is as charming as the smile designed to get a *yes* from me. He left out the part where I never see him again, but that's how it would end.

At least I'd be prepared for it. And it *would* be a fun night. We're obviously opposites, but there's definitely an attraction. If he even *semi-*delivers on the mind-blowing sex thing, it'd be better than the orgasmless wasteland I've been wandering the last six months.

"I agree to one date, but—" I point while narrowing my gaze. "With conditions."

His eyebrows rise and a twinkle lights his eyes. "Let's negotiate."

Ah, it's a businessman's twinkle. Our date, the one I've barely agreed to, is now a deal to be made. Harrison isn't the romantic match I'm waiting for, but he's clearly passionate. I might as well use that to my benefit.

"You'll choose the restaurant, I'll meet you there, and we'll split the check. You'll wear condoms, which you'll provide. Orgasms will be one-for-one, so if you're not able to deliver, prepare to go without. I won't text or call you afterward, and you won't tell a soul about this agreement."

His smile is the widest I've seen yet, filled with perfect pearly whites. Impeccable, like everything else about his appearance. "It's a good proposal, but I need to change a couple of the terms."

"Sorry, the 'satisfaction guaranteed' clause isn't negotiable." I've never been this forward. Or this saucy. I've always held back with the men I've dated, out of fear they'd hightail it to the door. That's not a worry with Harrison, and it's...liberating. "I'm great in bed, by the way, so the problem won't be on my end. If you don't think you can live up to your obligations—"

"Making you come won't be an obligation, Eden. It'll be my absolute fucking pleasure."

My knees buckle a little, and I grip the table's edge to steady myself. The F-word sounds really good rolling off his tongue. A tongue I'm now imagining between my legs. Heat blazes in his eyes as he openly checks out my body. There's a wolf inside his tailored suit, and I can't wait to see if he bites. By the time our gazes meet again, I'm ready to skip the fancy dinner and go straight to the part where he fulfills his nonobligatory orgasm delivery. The glint in his eyes tells me my desire is written all over my face. At this point, I don't even care.

"I'll send a car to pick you up and I'm paying the check. You'll have two orgasms, minimum, for each one I do. And I plan to use plenty of the condoms I'm providing, so rest up, sweetheart, because it's going to be a long night."

No mention of the no-further-contact portion of our deal, meaning he agrees to it. My romantic heart tightens a little, but it can take a backseat for one night.

"Deal," I say, sticking out my hand.

He shakes his head. "That's not how we seal *this* deal, sweetheart." He's in my personal space before I can draw breath. One palm splayed over the small of my back, he tugs me against his solid warmth. He cups my nape, holds me in place as he dips his head to mine.

My eyelids flutter closed at the tease of lips against lips. The barest touch, just enough to feel the warmth of his breath mingling with mine. I can't remember the last time I felt this thrilled for a first kiss. For any kiss.

"It's a deal." The words are a wisp across my lips, then he releases me, smiling as he retreats. "I'll send the details to your office, Ms. Greene. Thank you for making this an unexpectedly great night."

Then he's gone. And I'm alone, dateless and not being kissed, on Valentine's Day.

chapter
three

HARRISON

GREG and I have been best friends since meeting in high school. Roommates throughout post-secondary, despite going to different campuses. Even through the pressure-cooker of our multiple degree programs, being broke-ass entrepreneurs, then becoming wildly successful rich-ass entrepreneurs, we've never had a disagreement. Never kept secrets. Never lied.

So, when Greg walks into my office the Monday after Valentine's Day and asks, "How'd it go? Meet anyone interesting?" I'm in one hell of a sticky position.

"It wasn't as bad as I expected." It's evasion, not a lie. "But your MatchMakers membership is safe. Once was enough for me, I'm not interested in going back."

"Huh. I'm not saying they only accept ten-out-of-tens, but I've never seen an unattractive woman yet. I thought somebody might have interested you." He drops into the chair across from me, picks up a pen and begins doodling on my desk blotter. The guy is never motionless. "Nobody caught your eye?"

It's my silence that gives me away. I always have an answer.

"You *did* meet someone!" A hoot and a hand slap later, he's on his feet, leaning over my desk. "You met someone at a speed-dating event, and it burns your ass having to admit it."

"Are you done?"

"Not a chance, buddy." His continued hooting and geeky dance moves attract the attention of my secretary, who takes one look, then retreats to her desk in the outer office. "You know, I wasn't sure you'd actually go to the meetup. And I was kind of worried you'd behave like a jackoff if you did go."

Accurate concerns, since both things crossed my mind. "I wouldn't do anything to fuck you over, man. No matter how lame your method of meeting women is."

"Says the guy who used that lame method to meet someone Saturday night."

"I met lots of people in the speed-dating round. Didn't feel enough interest to match with any of them."

"But you said—"

"Nothing. You assumed."

He drops into the chair again, this time with a heavy sigh. "Wishful assuming. There's got to be a woman for you out there."

"There's a hell of a lot more than one," I say, laughing.

"You're really okay spending the rest of your life constantly hooking up with different women?"

I look away from my computer to raise my eyebrows at him. "How's that even a question? It's not torture, man. The opposite."

Greg grunts and shakes his head. "Nope. I want to go home to one person. Someone who cares about more than what my dick can do for her. A woman who loves me for me, the way I'll feel about her."

I'll never convince Greg that true love is bullshit. His rose-colored glasses are a permanent fixture. Poor guy's destined to a life of perpetual heartbreak and disappointment.

"I hope you find her one day." I'm not lying to him. I just know it won't happen.

"I will." The confidence in his voice is unmistakable. He's as sure about finding Mrs. Right as he is about his techie stuff. It's admirable, despite being misguided. "All right, back to work," he says, pushing up from the chair. He's halfway across the room when he turns to face me. "Hey, what did you think of Eden?"

My fingers freeze on the keyboard, but this time, I'm quick enough to answer. "The MatchMaker woman?"

"Yeah. Did you have a chance to talk to her?"

I nod. "When I checked in and out." Still not lying. I should leave it at that, but curiosity gets the best of me. "Why?"

"She's the reason I go to the events."

Oh fuck. Should've kept my mouth shut. Now I've got to see it through, even if it means I have to cancel the only date I've been truly excited about in years. "Got a crush on the pretty cupid, do you?"

"What? No. She's hot, and very nice, but she's too sweet. I need someone with a bit of fire."

It takes all my self-control not to laugh. Apparently, my friend and I have met two different versions of Eden Greene. "Then why's she the reason you keep going back for more unsuccessful matchmaking?"

"You're hilarious," he says, rolling his eyes. "It's not unsuccessful. I've connected with all the matches I've made. None of them have been *the* one, but I'm getting closer to finding her. Eden's the best matchmaker in the city. Bet I'm walking down the aisle with soon-to-be Mrs. Right before the end of the year."

"If Eden is such a great matchmaker, why is she still single?" The dig is out of my mouth before my good sense kicks in. All I can do is hope it slides under the radar.

Greg's eyebrows disappear into his shaggy mop of computer-geek hair. "How do you know she's single?"

Shit. Busted. My lack of a snappy comeback—hell, of any comeback—isn't helping. Each second of silence further seals my fate. Short of outright lying, I'm fucked.

"Eden is the woman who caught your eye." A shit-eating grin stretches across his face. "The world's biggest love cynic falls for the queen of happily-ever-after. This might be the best news ever."

"It's not news, and I didn't fall for her. Attraction isn't love. It's a precursor to lust. A temporary physiological reaction to someone who could be sexually compatible. Attraction is like a lit match—a big, hot flame that burns out. Then you light a new one."

"Well, it's good you believe that," he says, laughing on his way across the room.

I must be a glutton for punishment, but I can't help myself from asking, "Why?"

"Because you won't be heartbroken when you can't land Eden Greene."

"I don't want to *land* her." Would I like to strip her naked and enjoy every sexy inch? Hell yes. But I will set her free afterward.

Free to find another man to share her saucy mouth

with. To share her body with. A man who'll make her forget I ever existed.

Shit.

Greg pauses in my office doorway. "Hang on, I need to capture this moment," he says, pulling out his phone and taking my picture.

"What moment is that—the moment before I kick your ass out of my office, or maybe just kick your ass?"

He's still sporting the damn grin. If anything, it's grown wider. "The moment you realized you're at risk of falling in love." He's out of sight before I can hit him with a smartass response.

Annoying bastard. Let him think what he wants, I know he's wrong. I'll never fall in love. Not even with Eden Greene.

HARRISON

I've checked the table and ordered wine. Now I'm in front of the restaurant, my attention tuned to the back-and-forth slide of Saturday evening traffic. A section of curbside space is cordoned off for valet parking and limo services. Two traditional stretches have pulled up while I've been waiting, but it's the sleek, black Rolls Royce that draws me to the curb.

I told her I'd send a car. Based on our back-and-forth emails this week, I think she expects an Uber. I would've loved to see the expression on her face when the Rolls arrived.

"I've got it." I press some folded bills into the driver's

palm when he comes around to open the rear passenger door.

His reply, along with everything else, becomes unimportant background noise the moment I open the car door. The world is full of beautiful women, but none of them hold a candle to the one smiling up at me. It's not just her face. More than her body. There's something about her that reaches inside me and flips a switch. Turns me on in ways that are more than sexual.

"You look stunning," I say, offering my hand. Every nerve ending in my body is on high alert the second her soft skin glides against mine.

"Thank you. You look quite dapper."

"Dapper. Haven't heard that word since I spent summer holidays with my grandparents as a kid."

"Good memories?" she asks, as I place my palm on the small of her back to guide her toward the entrance.

"Some of the best."

She pauses before we reach the door. Her gaze takes in the building's meticulous façade before she turns to face me. "Are we here because this is your favorite restaurant?"

"They have the best chateaubriand in the city and the sommelier has a few vintages you literally can't get anywhere else."

"That was the most pompous non-answer I've ever heard." There she is, the woman I haven't stopping thinking about since last Saturday night.

I feel my smile stretch into a grin. "It's a great restaurant, but not my favorite."

"*Much* better answer," she says, pressing a manicured finger to my chest.

"You want to ditch this place and go to my favorite?" Shit, that came out of nowhere. I'm a planner. Always several moves ahead. Tonight's date is no different—-*was* no different. Now I'm flying blind. But damn, if the view ahead isn't full of living color.

Her perfect, dark eyebrows rise, and an equally perfect smile follows. "I'd love that."

"Let's do it."

Her laughter fills the air as I take her hand, still grinning like a monkey while leading her in the opposite direction. "Don't you have to cancel the reservation?"

"They can send me a bill." One arm in the air to flag a cab as we reach the curb, I take in her form-fitting lavender dress, and tilt my head. "You can send me your dry-cleaning bill, too."

"Are things going to get messy?"

"Bet on it."

"Do you bet on everything?" she asks, as I open the rear door of the first taxi to stop.

"Only on things I'm sure I'll win." I usher her inside, then slide in beside her. "Steeles and Forty-Seventh."

She blinks her pretty eyes at me. "That's your office's address."

"It's also home of the best food truck in the city."

"Your favorite restaurant is a food truck below your office?"

"You'll understand once you've tasted Stan's burgers. He has a vegan version if you don't do meat."

"Well, I have been living the meatless life for several months, but only because there hasn't been any quality sausage available. I'm hopeful that'll change tonight."

My burst of gut-deep laughter draws the cabbie's attention. But he's irrelevant. Everything is, aside from Eden.

"No hope required, sweetheart. You won't go to sleep hungry tonight."

She wiggles closer and places her hand high enough on my leg to trigger an immediate increase in blood flow to my cock. "You do look quite dapper in this suit. I've never dated a man with meatballs big enough to wear a maroon suit, but you pull it off."

"Thanks." I'm still grinning like a madman. I can't remember the last time I smiled this much on a date, and we're only at the beginning.

The stoplights are in sync tonight, and we're close to our destination after ten minutes of good conversation. I wouldn't mind a bit of time to walk with her, so I lean forward to address the cabbie. "This is good, thanks."

He pulls over just shy of the original target. I pay the fare and tip, thank him, then escort Eden from the cab. Taking her hand feels natural, and the smile she gives me when I do feels like a gold star on a test I didn't know I was taking.

Saucy Eden is sexy as fuck, I definitely want her to come back out and play. But this glimpse of her soft side is addictive too. I have a feeling there are a lot of layers to this woman, and I wouldn't mind seeing more. A lot more. More than there's time for on one date.

The world's biggest love cynic falls for the queen of happily-ever-after. Greg's unwelcome voice invades my happy thoughts.

"Mosquito?" she asks, when I shake my head to clear my friend's antagonizing words.

"Some kind of bug." *And his name is Greg.* "It's gone."

"That's good. I hate fighting bugs off while I'm eating." She cranes her neck and peers up and down the street. "Where is this food truck, anyway?"

"Around the corner, tucked into a cut-through between a couple buildings."

"Are you sure it's going to be open on a Saturday night? This isn't exactly a nightlife district."

"Not the kind you can see." I use our joined hands to point upward at the office buildings looming above. "Stan knows all the workaholics' schedules. He'll be open."

"And you know this because you're one of the Saturday-night workaholics?"

"Sometimes." I chuckle when she gives me a disbelieving glance. "Okay, most times." I squeeze her hand. "But I'm glad I got booted out of the office last Saturday."

"Me too."

Stan hails us with a wave the moment we enter his view. "Ah, and who is this lovely creature who's unchained you from your desk for the evening?"

"This is Eden Greene, the city's most in-demand matchmaker."

"A pleasure." Stan tips his cap and bends at the waist. "A matchmaker, eh? Do you have anybody who'd be interested in an overfed, well-seasoned burger flipper?"

"I'm sure we could find you a perfect match."

"Ah, to be a young romantic again," the gray-haired man says, chuckling while donning a fresh pair of gloves. "I know what Harrison wants. What can I make for you, Miss Greene?"

"Hmm…" Her profile is as beautiful as every other angle, and I'm caught staring when she abandons the menu board to meet my eyes. "I'll have the messiest burger you make, Stan."

"Two loaded skyscrapers, coming right up."

The sizzle of fresh patties on the grill and clanging of

various implements fills the evening air. From experience, I know Stan's whistling some made-up tune while he cooks, but I'll be damned if I hear a single note.

Everything's out of focus, except Eden. Each second I look at her, I feel lighter, like a weight's lifting. A weight I didn't realize was there. It's like breathing fresh air after holding your breath for too long.

I need to get control. If I keep looking at her this way, I'm going to forget why we're here. One date. That's what she agreed to.

"You may have bitten off more than you can chew with that order," I say.

"Don't worry, I'll get it all in my mouth somehow."

My gaze drops to that mouth, and it takes everything I've got not to groan aloud. Those lips will be wrapped around my cock later. Part of me can't fucking wait. A bigger part of me doesn't want to rush to the bedroom portion of our date, because then our one night together would be over.

I need to get out of my head. Focus on the physical. It's pheromones and physiology, I'm not falling for her. I barely know anything about her. That's how it's going to stay.

Yet when I open my mouth to serve up an innuendo-laden comeback, "Tell me how you got into the matchmaking business," are the words that come out.

"I'd rather not."

I couldn't ask for a better opportunity to circle back to our flirtatious bantering. But I don't take it. "I asked because I'm genuinely interested."

"And I'm genuinely not interested in sharing that information with you."

After my comments last weekend, I had that coming. Regret's not a familiar flavor for me, but there's no mistaking its taste. "I don't believe in true love and happily-ever-after, but I wouldn't say a negative word about your business."

"Emotions and business decisions are separate things for you. They're intertwined for me, and unraveling them isn't the kind of messy either of us is looking for tonight."

Shit. I'm fucking this up. I never fuck things up, and more to the point, I don't want to. Not with her. "All right, tell me something else about yourself—wait, let's do this your way."

"My way?" she asks, tilting her head. Adorable. Still sexy as fuck, but adorable.

Time to prove I was paying attention last Saturday. Because I was. Every single word and gesture she made. "What's the strangest food you've ever tried?"

Her eyes open wide, her pretty mouth opening to an O that would fit my cock quite nicely. "That's a sample question from the MatchMaker's event."

I nod. "Are any of them off-limits, or am I allowed to ask them all?"

"They're not off-limits, but...why bother asking?"

"I want to get to know you. I'm interested in you, Eden. Your mind, your spirit. Those attracted me just as much as your beautiful face and sexy body."

Her lips twist and her gaze flits over my face before narrowing and settling on my eyes again. "We made a deal about tonight, and I don't want to back out of it. But I will, if you use your playbook pickup lines on me."

"I haven't, and I won't. Our date is different. No games, no lines. We can be honest and straightforward, no phoniness or lies. Just be ourselves, knowing there's no judgment, and it's going to be a great time."

"Wow," she says, a throaty noise accompanying her slight head shake. "You described my ideal date."

"I never stopped to think about what my ideal date would look like, but now that you've said that, I agree." I lean in close, and press a soft kiss below her earlobe. "Thanks for being my perfect date."

Her breath hitches as I brush my lips across hers while retreating, her eyebrows pinching together when I resume my former position without taking the kiss further.

"I can't kiss you here. I want to, but I can't."

"Because we're near your office?"

I shake my head. "Because we're not near my bed."

"It's just a kiss," she says, smiling and leaning in to nudge my shoulder with hers.

"I've known since the first time you spoke to me that kissing you would never be 'just a kiss.'"

No saucy retort leaves her parted lips. No answer of any kind. She heard more than flirty words—and she didn't hear wrong. She just stares at me, the power of her beautiful amber eyes stripping away another layer from the wall I've spent my adult lifetime building.

"Hey, lovebirds—burgers up!"

"That's us," I say, squeezing her hand. A week ago, I would've scoffed at the term *lovebirds*. Mocked it openly. Now... I'm not so sure.

chapter
four

EDEN

WE HAVEN'T HAD a sip of alcohol tonight, yet my head is spinning as if I'm drunk when we tumble through the door of Harrison's condo, laughing to the point of having stomach cramps. We also haven't had our first kiss yet.

There's been lots of contact. Harrison is a hands-on kind of guy, I've discovered. Always touching me, whether it's holding my hand, resting his palm on my back, stroking my nape. That last one made me tingle, which didn't go unnoticed, based on his wolfish smile. He has an arsenal of smiles, and I admit to liking them all. A lot. But I'd like to see that wolfish one again. Preferably while we're naked.

That's why I'm here—for the sex. The fact that I've had the most fun in—well, forever—doing non-sex things with him tonight is just a bonus. It's okay if I like him. The sex will be even better because I do. But that's still all this is— one fun night to take the edge off. I just need to keep my romantic heart safely locked up for a few more hours. The way he's acting tonight isn't making that easy.

"I still can't believe you've never been go-karting before tonight." Harrison circles my waist from behind, pulling my body tight to his while walking us through his semi-lit, fourteenth-floor unit. "You drove like a Formula One professional and a smash-up derby champ, rolled into one."

"And I can't believe *that's* your favorite recreational activity."

"Second favorite." His words slide into my ear like a velvety promise as he skims one hand over my abdomen, halting his descent when his fingertips graze the top of my mound. "Been thinking about enjoying my favorite since the moment I laid eyes on you."

Good thing he's controlling our forward motion, because everything from my knees down turns to jelly when we enter the bedroom. "Can I shower first? I'm sweaty and kind of grimy from go-karting."

"That's our first stop, sweetheart."

"Our?" My heart pounds harder as we continue past the massive bed, into an en suite bathroom that could be the feature in a modern decorating magazine. Everything is glossy white and gray, including the walk-in shower that's larger than the entire bathroom in my basement apartment. "Are we showering together?"

"We both want to clean up, but I have two bathrooms. You can use this one." He places a soft kiss on my shoulder before releasing me. "Feel free to open any cabinet or drawer, nothing's off-limits, use whatever you want. Take your time, and call me if you need anything."

"Okay," I say, and he smiles, then walks away. A gentleman. The one I'll be giving my body to very soon, so... "I thought of something I need."

He turns, waits for whatever thing I'm about to request. Whatever it is, he's probably prepared for it.

"Help with my zipper?"

"Of course." He's behind me again in two strides, his breath tickling my neck as he carefully slides the zipper downward, from the top of my spine, to the cleavage of my ass. "Anything else?" Huskiness laces his voice. His hand lingers where the zipper ended, his fingertips grazing the newly revealed bare skin.

It's the lightest touch, but it sets me on fire. And I want to burn out of control. "Yes. Unhook my bra." I hold my breath as his hands rise to the band.

"It's a front hook."

"Yes, it is." I like being this forward, this uninhibited. I could get used to it.

He pushes my dress forward, off my shoulders. An impatient growl vibrates against my neck when the dress refuses to freely slide from my body.

I bite my lip to suppress a giggle, only to have a gasp rush out when he grips the defiant dress and tugs it all the way down.

Then his hands are on my body, leaving a trail of heated sparks as he slides them up to my breasts. A quick flick and the clasp opens. Just as quickly, the bra joins my dress in a puddle on the floor.

"What else do you need?" he asks, cupping my breasts from behind.

I can barely think with his thumbs stroking my nipples, but I focus enough to find the words. "Take off my panties."

The last slip of lace is gone before I can take another breath. Then my ability to breathe disappears altogether, as his fingers slip between my legs.

"Fuck, you're so soft." He pulls my earlobe into his mouth, teasing it with his tongue as he slides his finger inside me. "And so fucking wet. I don't think you can wait for a shower."

"I can't."

"Then I'll ask again, so you can be just as specific as your other answers." He withdraws from my pussy to focus on my clit. "What do you need?"

"I need to come," I whisper.

"Are you asking me to get you a vibrator?"

My head falls back as he increases the speed of his circles. "No."

"Then what do you need, sweetheart?" His voice is so close to my ear, it vibrates straight to my core. "No judgment, remember? No holding back. Nothing's off-limits."

"Make me come."

He answers with a growl against my neck. With his fingers, rubbing my clit hard and fast. With his arm wrapped so tightly around me, it squeezes the air from my lungs. "I'm going to make you come so many times tonight. With my hands, my tongue, my cock. Everything you ever wanted, I'm giving it to you."

White flashes behind my closed eyelids as the spiral hits. I grab his arm and shoulder, desperately hanging on as I ride his relentless, masterful fingers through an orgasm that leaves me panting.

"I need that shower," I say, once the ability to speak returns. "And I want you in there with me."

"Done." He's not a huge guy, but he sweeps me off my feet effortlessly.

Arms twined behind his neck, I kick off my heels, and push my fingers through the short, brown hair that's as thick and soft as it looks. "I also need you to kiss me. No more excuses."

He grunts a laugh. "Excuses? It's been torture not kissing you tonight."

"Then you should have. I kept thinking you were going to, then you didn't."

"I told you why I couldn't." He sets me on the ground at the shower's edge, his heated gaze traveling over my body as he undresses. Suit jacket, shirt, and tie—gone. Tossed aside as if they were rags. "Remember when I nearly kissed you last weekend?"

"Vividly."

He chuckles while unbuckling his belt. "Same, sweetheart. I knew once I had a taste of you, I wouldn't want to stop." He unzips his pants, hooks his fingers under the band of whatever underwear he favors. He pushes his remaining clothes off simultaneously, leaving him gloriously, mouthwateringly naked. "If I would've kissed you after wiping the mustard off the corner of your mouth tonight, or when you pressed your tits against my arm on the way to the go-kart track, I would've ordered the cabbie to head straight here."

"That wouldn't have been horrible," I say, unable to take my eyes off his long, thick cock.

He chuckles again, the depth of it caressing the shell of my ear as he walks me backward, into the shower. "When I said I want to do everything with you tonight, I meant everything, including hearing you laugh, watching your gorgeous, joyful smile, for every minute I could."

My silly heart skips a couple beats, but that's as far as I'll let it wander. I know he's sincere. He's a romantic, absolutely. Just a serial one.

He reaches for the faucets, and I brace myself for a blast of cold water that doesn't come. The temperature is instantly hot as it hits us from multiple showerheads.

"Good?" he asks, glancing at me over his shoulder.

"Perfect."

Smiling, he winds one nicely muscled arm around my waist and tugs me tight to him, with his cock trapped between us. His other hand releases my hair from its upsweep, then he wraps the length around his hand and tilts my head back. "Time for my first taste of Eden."

I've never wanted to be kissed so badly in my life, and he doesn't disappoint. The first press of his lips steals my breath. Perfect pressure, perfect fit. The prowess of his tongue as he strokes into my mouth. I'm on fire again, grabbing his firm butt, trying to hook my leg around his hip. Forget sensibility and safety, I want his cock between my legs. Inside my body. And I know how to get it.

"I need you to fuck me."

He groans against my mouth, nips my bottom lip. "Soon." He gives my ass a smack, then puts space between us. "Have to get rid of the sweat," he says, lathering his lean, muscular body with a body wash I'll need to steal when I leave. "I've been thinking about burying my cock in your sexy mouth all week."

"Just in my mouth?"

"No." His eyes darken as I soap myself, his gaze tracking my hands as I pay extra attention to unnecessarily cleaning my breasts. "Fuck, you're beautiful." The Adam's apple slides up and down his throat as I trail my hands downward.

"Where else did you think about burying your cock?" Touching my clit is a mistake when I'm this turned-on. With his eyes glued to my ministrations, I can't *not* touch myself. My hips jut forward instinctively, and a soft moan escapes my lips. "Here?" I ask, sliding two fingers back and forth.

"Yeah, right there, baby." Water sluices over his skin as he palms his cock. "Turn around, and I'll tell you where else I'm going to bury this cock you're eyeing."

My breathing stutters, but I do as he says. "Where else?" I ask, looking over my shoulder to meet his hungry gaze.

In a blink, he's right behind me, his hard cock nestled in the valley between my cheeks. "When you're ready, sweetheart, and only then, I'm going to bury every inch in your perfect ass."

I'm shaking, and it has nothing to do with cold, or fear. I've tried anal before, more than once. I know I can handle it, physically, but I didn't love it. That hasn't stopped me from fantasizing about it. From wanting it with the right person. Everything in me says Harrison is that person—and not just for anal.

I can't think about that right now. I push my heart back into its safety box and focus on the very hot sex I'm about to have. "How will you know when I'm ready?"

He curls his fingers around my hips. Skates one hand across my abdomen and finds my clit again. "Because you'll spread your pretty round cheeks and tell me you *need* my cock in your ass."

Could I say that? With Harrison, yes, even though I've never been that sexually bold. I've always held back, given in to all my "what if" worries. What if he doesn't like doing what I suggested? What if I look bad from that angle? What if he thinks I'm a freak and never calls again? I've always settled. And it's never enough. Tonight will be different. It already is.

chapter
five

HARRISON

I **MADE** big promises about tonight, and I'll keep them. With fucking pleasure, literally. But goddamn, if I don't get inside her soon...

"Take me to bed."

"Done." I hit the faucets without looking. Grab an oversized bath towel from the shelf and wrap it around both of us, because I'm not giving up touching her for one more second.

It's a short walk to my bed, but still too damn far. My craving for Eden is unlike anything I've experienced. I wasn't exaggerating when I told her I'd lose control once I got a taste. My dick feels like it's filled with steel and I'm actually salivating at the thought of burying my face between her legs. There aren't enough hours left in one night for all the things I want to do to her. I need more time. A lot more.

She stops at the edge of the bed, the towel dropping to

the floor as she turns in my arms. "You've got everything covered, right?"

"As promised, and more. I'll take care of everything, sweetheart. Leave it to me and just enjoy." The condoms are an extra precaution. We exchanged test results via email, we're both clean, and I know she's on the Pill. I'll still suit up before I fuck her, but the peace of mind means we can safely play. The tests were her idea, and I was one-hundred-percent on board. Honestly, it just made me like her more. Everything does.

"I need you to fuck me."

"I need that too. But I need you to come first." I trail my fingers down her back, through the crack of her sexy ass, then hitch her leg up, over my hip. My cock is trapped between us, and I rock the shaft back and forth against her clit until her bottom lip falls and her eyelids flutter closed.

She's close, I can see it. Hear it. Fuck, I can smell it. I need to taste it.

She gasps as I scoop her up, then again when I lay her out on her back, with her legs spread wide.

"Ask me what I need," I say, settling between her creamy thighs.

"What do you need?" Her voice is a husky whisper that's going to star in every jerking-off fantasy I have, for the rest of my life.

"I need to lick your sweet pussy until you come all over my face." I hold eye contact while taking my first long, slow taste. That's it for my control. I'm a starving man with a feast in front of me, and I am all-fucking-in.

The room's filled with her soft moans. A bite of pain shoots through me from her fingernails, where she's got a fistful of my hair, holding me in place, as if there's anywhere else in this world I'd rather be than right here, eating her sweet pussy.

Her hips buck off the bed, and her legs tense beside my ears. I double down on her sweet clit, flicking and sucking every last ripple of heaving orgasm from her perfect pussy.

I take a last lick when she's wriggling from sensitivity, then kiss my way up her body. Her tits are incredible, but I keep moving. I need her mouth beneath mine. And I need inside her.

I roll away long enough to grab a condom. Maybe five seconds. A blink, in the grand scheme. But the instant I turn toward her, I'm blindsided. "Fuck, you're beautiful."

"You know I'm a sure thing at this point, right?" Her smile, her eyes, they're so bright, they take my breath away.

And I'm not a man who gives up his oxygen easily.

I tear the package and roll on the condom, cover her with my body, and slide home. I hiss through gritted teeth as Eden's pussy hugs me. Fucking squeezes me. "You're so tight. Am I hurting you?"

"No, God no." Her legs wrap around my hips, opening her wider. "Fuck me deeper, I need you to fuck me hard."

Mating urge, engaged. One arm braced against the headboard and one banded under her ass, I rise up so I can give her what she needs. What we both need. I pull out and fill her fast and deep, fucking her hard enough to make her tits bounce. So fucking sexy.

Her face is rosy, her eyes heavy-lidded with lusty oblivion. She's close, but not there. I need her to get there. Soon, because each stroke takes me closer to a line I won't be able to go back from.

I grab her hand, place it between her legs, then brace against the headboard again. "Show me how you make yourself come."

Her cheeks burn deep red, but her fingers start moving. Back and forth, back and forth, harder and faster, until she's gasping the sexiest little noises I've ever fucking heard. Her hips tip higher and everything clenches, including her pussy.

I couldn't stop now if my life depended on it. "Fuuuck..." I bury myself to the balls and unload before folding myself over her like a possessive, rutting beast.

"Can't...breathe..."

Shit. "Can't kill you, I'm not done with you," I say, rolling onto my back.

She shrieks when I take her along for the ride. "I'm loving this deal so far," she says, resting her cheek on my chest.

The deal. One night—a good dinner, fun conversation, mind-blowing sex with a two-to-one orgasm ratio. She's right, so far, I've delivered. We both have. Only it stopped feeling like an arrangement to me the minute I opened that car door. But not to her, apparently.

"Fuck."

Her head pops up, and she smiles at me while digging her chin into my sternum. "Again? Okay."

I grunt a laugh because she's adorable, and because it's expected. "Soon. Definitely soon. Unfortunately, I have to check on something first." I slip free of her body, leaning over for another taste of her sweet lips before heading for the bathroom.

"Do you have to go out? Should I get dressed?"

"Stay naked. I'm just going to duck into my home office for a few minutes, then I'll be ready to pick up where we left off."

"Deal," she says, after I've kissed her again.

I smile until I'm out of sight. Hold my shit together

until I'm safely entrenched behind my small desk. I exhale, closing my eyes as I push my fingers through my hair. The same hair Eden gripped to pull my face against her pussy not that many minutes ago. If I hadn't left her alone in my bed, she could be doing that again, right now.

My cock twitches inside the boxers I threw on. The blood is headed south, because my body's ready and willing to uphold my end of *the deal*. Give Eden as much filthy-good sex as we can cram into one night. Then goodbye. No further obligations, no fizzling-out period, no breakup. It's a great fucking deal. And I want to break it.

It could be even better. The sex is already amazing, and we've barely scratched the surface. Even if we have the stamina to cover all the bases tonight, I'm pretty damn sure we're going to want to cover them again. Many times.

There's more to it than sex though. Has been since the beginning, if I'm honest. That switch that flipped inside me earlier—she was toggling that switch from minute one.

We can fuck until dawn, but it won't be enough. I want to watch her eat breakfast. Hear more of her stories. Carry her back to bed and brunch on her sweet pussy, then spend the day doing whatever makes her laugh. Fuck, I'm already mentally planning next weekend. The one after that. Six more after that.

Until Eden, the furthest out I'd plan is my escape. Now that's the last thing on my mind.

The world's biggest love cynic falls for the queen of happily-ever-after. This might be the best news ever. Greg's words make another appearance in my mind, and this time, I'm not laughing. Not kicking him to the curb, either.

The dimmed light is still on when I return to the bedroom, and it's enough for me to see Eden tucked under the covers. She's curled on her side, eyes closed, lips slightly parted. Fast asleep. My beautiful, sexy, perfectly filthy angel.

If I thought this would be our only night together, I'd slide in behind her and wake her up in a way that'd tick another box of our deal. We're going to have more nights. A lot more. I slide in behind her, wrap my arms around her and gently nuzzle her hair, then let her sleepy breathing take me along with it.

HARRISON

The Sunday morning sun beaming through my window hits me squarely in the face. It's better than an alarm clock, that's why I never pull the blinds at night. Sleeping in is for suckers. Staying in bed with my beauty isn't the worst idea in the world though. My beauty. That's a first. And a last, because she's the only one I want to think of as mine.

I roll to my other side, and—she's not there. The sheets are rumpled but cool. There's no noise coming from the bathroom, and when I sit up and crane my neck to see farther into the en suite, her clothes are missing from the floor.

Maybe she's not a lounge-in-bed person. It wouldn't surprise me. You don't become a business owner—especially in a city full of them—without the drive to get up and go. She's probably sitting at my kitchen island, drumming her fingernails on the granite, wondering when I'm going to haul my ass out of bed and join her in the land of the living.

I'll do that now. Then I'll drag her back to bed so we can

warm up those sheets again. I scrub my hands over my cheeks and finger-comb my hair on my way to the bedroom door. It's closed, and I left it open last night. Maybe she's a super-early morning person, and didn't want to wake me.

I don't know much day-to-day stuff about her yet. That'll come. Until then, I know how to make *her* come, and I'm ready to put that knowledge to use again. Pretty sure she'll be on board with that plan.

The smile I'm sporting becomes an audible, "What the hell?" when I step out of the bedroom. The condo's main area is open concept, and she's nowhere to be seen. "Eden?" I feel like an idiot, calling her name. I do it anyway. Pointlessly, because the place isn't that big, and she's obviously not here. I check the guest room, office, and second bathroom anyway. All empty.

It's barely past six, and she's gone. No note left behind. She's just gone.

Did she think this is what I wanted? Probably. We didn't discuss spending the night, and at no point did I suggest she stay. I just assumed she would, the way I assume everything will fall into place. I should've known better than to assume anything with Eden. She's surprised me at every turn.

It's my turn to surprise her, with words I never thought I'd say.

chapter
six

EDEN

KNOCKING from my front door sends my cat scurrying under the side table. The pussy is a pussy. Though he's not wrong to be on alert, I'm not expecting company or a delivery on a Sunday morning. It's probably someone with the wrong address. All the brownstones in my row are identical, and there are enough doors to make it very confusing.

I can't see my door from my living room window, so I grab my pepper spray from the hall table on my way. I squint and press my face to the peephole, jumping back when I see who's on the other side.

Why is he here? I'm positive I didn't leave anything in his condo. Okay, a piece of my heart I couldn't save, and a big bunch of inhibitions, yes, but nothing tangible. Even if I had, it wouldn't be anything that required immediate or personal return.

He can't see in, yet I plaster myself to the wall when he knocks a second time. I'm not ready to face him yet.

Honestly, not ever. Whatever this is, it isn't part of our deal.

My phone rings inside my pocket, and I nearly jump out of my skin. In my scramble to silence it, it slips from my hands, clattering on the tile while belting out two more noisy rings. Maybe he didn't hear it, or he'll think he has the wrong apartment.

"Eden." My name accompanies another knock. "I know you're in there, that was me calling you."

I tap the screen. *Missed Call—Harrison.*

For him to come all the way over here, and break our no-call-the-day-after agreement, it must be important.

I give myself a onceover and shrug. It doesn't matter what he thinks of my Sunday comfies. It doesn't matter what he thinks about anything. *Liar.* I need to get it together, so I don't fall apart when he's looking in my eyes. I can't let him see what he means to me. What he *meant* to me, because the deal ended when I walked out of his condo.

I inhale, stuff my heart back into its safe place, and open the door. "Wow. You own clothes that aren't suits." Sass is the only way I'll survive being face-to-face with him. All other forms of communication are too dangerous.

"A few things," he says, chipping at my defenses with his smile.

"What are you doing here?" The sooner I find out, the sooner I can put him, and our perfect night together, in my memory box, and move on.

"You were gone when I woke up."

"I had to get home for my cat. He's not used to being alone at night." *Because I am.*

"I didn't know you have a cat. You didn't mention it."

"I didn't mention a lot of things. The speed-dating sample questions don't cover everything." I hate the bitterness in my voice. This is what we were supposed to avoid. Emotions I wasn't supposed to have to feel. "I'm sorry for being a bitch. You just...aren't supposed to be here."

"You were asleep when I came back to the bedroom, then gone when I woke up. We didn't have a chance to talk."

"I told you I didn't expect you to call the next day. That was part of the one-date deal."

"I want a new deal." He steps closer, filling the doorframe, one hand on each side. "I need to see you again."

"I'm not interested in being anyone's fuck buddy, even yours."

"I'd never expect that from you. That's not what I want." The wood squeaks beneath his grip as he exhales, long and low. "Fuck, I don't know how to do this."

"Then it's probably not natural, and you shouldn't try to make it be."

"You think people can't change if they try?" His eyes are so clear, it's as if he's opened the gates for me to see straight through to his soul.

It's a good soul. One I could love forever, if he were a man who wanted to be loved. That's not who he is, and the sooner I say goodbye to him, the less it will hurt when he's gone.

"I think we're programmed the way we're programmed. But we're not like the video games you make, we can't simply be reprogrammed to fit a new market." I step closer and touch his face. I can't resist, especially when he leans into the contact. "I know I can't change, Harrison."

He catches my wrist before I can back away, and pulls

me into his arms. "I'm not asking you to change. I'm asking you to give me a chance, to see if I can."

"Why would you want to?"

"Because I like you, Eden. A lot. Every minute I'm with you, I like you more."

"You didn't like the other women you dated? That doesn't paint you in a great light."

His laugh is so genuine, it forces a smile to my face. "Yes, I liked them, I'm not a complete asshole. But it was shallow liking. In both directions, not just mine. It's different with you. I'm different with you."

I wiggle free of his embrace, wrapping my arms around myself in a sad substitute for his hug. "The trouble is, I've been acting differently with you, too. The Eden you like so much isn't the real me."

"All the laughter, the opinions, the attitude—that was fake?"

"Not fake. Just...not the whole me. You asked why I started a matchmaking business. I'm a diehard romantic, and I don't want to be anything else. I grew up surrounded by lifelong happy couples. I believe in true love because I've witnessed it, multiple times. I want one of my own. Carefree, uninhibited Eden, the one you like so much—she doesn't worry about ruining her chance at a fairytale ending. She doesn't hold back because she's not afraid her heart might get broken. The whole me won't settle for less than a happily-ever-after."

"I'm not asking you to settle."

"I believe you want more time together. But another date or two won't be enough for me. I already like you too much. I'll fall in love with you, and you'll break my heart. Not intentionally, but you will, because we don't want the same things. I want to experience the great love of a lifetime. You don't even believe in it. I can't go down this road with you, knowing where it'll end."

I can't look at him anymore. Nor can I escape him, so I lean against the wall and let my head fall back against it. The door closes, and I snap my head up, expecting to be alone, but I'm not.

He's still here, in my apartment. In my personal space, as he brackets me between braced arms. "I grew up surrounded by divorce. My parents, uncles, aunts. My friends, as I got older. Love turned them into angry people with bitter hearts full of blame. I swore I'd never fall into that pattern. That I'd never end up that way."

Oh, my heart. "What about your grandparents? You said your memories with them were some of the best. Did they divorce, too?"

A fleeting smile crosses his face. "No. They were the exception. Loved each other unconditionally."

"Then you have seen true love. You know it's real."

"Until one of them dies. That's the worst heartbreak of all."

"I'm sorry." Touching him will make it harder to let go, but I wrap my arms around him anyway.

He pulls me tighter, presses his lips to my temple. "I've never told anyone those things."

"Thank you for trusting me." Cheek pressed to his warm, solid chest, I fight back the emotions threatening to break free of their safe place. "I appreciate you letting me in, even if only for a moment."

"It's not easy."

"I know."

He tightens his embrace when I try to ease free. "You're not the only one making choices to protect your heart. I just didn't realize that's what I was doing."

"Now that you know, what are you going to do?"

His embrace relaxes, and he tips my chin up with one hand. "I'm going to give you a chance to break it."

"I'd never want to do that."

"But you could. *You*, Eden. No one else."

"You barely know me," I whisper. Anything louder might stir more words to escape. Words that would rip the lid right off my heart's safekeeping box.

He shakes his head. "I don't know a lot *about* you. Yet."

I can't help smiling when he winks. "I haven't agreed to anything."

"Yet." He takes my hand, kisses it softly, then places it on his chest, over his heart. "This tells me I *know* you. You say I can't change, but the truth is, I don't want to change. The man you spent last night with—that's the real me. No pretense, no walls. I want to keep being that man. With you, for you, for—fuck, I never thought I'd say this. Never thought I'd want to say this. I want that for the rest of my life."

I don't think my heart could beat any faster. The lid isn't just off my emotional safety box, it's smashed to smithereens, leaving my heart unprotected. It's out, beating wildly, trying to force its way up my throat to confess the feelings I tried so hard not to have for this man.

I can't tell him. So I shake my head. Squeeze my eyes shut, because this can't be real. Not permanently.

"Hey." His velvety voice is gentle as he cups my face in both hands, stroking my cheeks with his thumbs. "Please look at me. Tell me what's going through your beautiful mind."

I meet his eyes, blinking fast, desperate to keep my tears in check. "I'm scared."

"That I'm full of shit? I'm telling you the truth, Eden. I've never been more honest in my life."

"You told me you don't believe in love."

"And you said you wouldn't go out with me if I were the last man alive. It wasn't a lie when either of us said those things, but our truths change. I want to be with you, Eden. Only you. That's my truth now."

"Until it changes again." My stomach knots when he exhales, clearly frustrated, then presses his forehead to mine. It's going to end in this hallway. Better now than a week or a month down the road. My heart is cracked open, but it can heal. More time with him will open it wider, and when he leaves for good, it'll shatter into a million unfixable pieces.

His face is so close, our noses touch, and our silent breathing mingles. I force my hands against the wall, fighting the urge to touch him. To pull him as close as I can, and lose myself in his steady warmth, the way I did last night.

"You can go. I don't expect...more. This isn't what you want."

He raises his head, bringing us face-to-face again. "Would I rather this were easy, that I'd walked in here, told you I love you, and you jumped straight into my arms? Of course that's what I wanted."

"You—" I shake my head. There's no way I heard correctly.

"At the MatchMaker's event, you asked if five minutes is enough to feel a spark of chemistry. I didn't need five minutes, it was instant with you. You asked if our true love could be in the room that night. I thought it was laughable, but mine was. I was just too pigheaded to realize it at the time."

"You were *so* pigheaded." I shake my head again, this time with a smile. "I liked you anyway, even though I tried not to."

"And I'm the luckiest pigheaded jerk in the world because of it."

"You're not a jerk. It would've been easier to leave this morning if you were," I say, giving in to temptation and tugging a fistful of his t-shirt.

He takes the opening, sliding his arms around my waist and pulling me close. "I hope it's never easy to leave me."

"You say that as if there's going to be another opportunity."

"There has to be. If you're not ready to say yes today, I'll try again tomorrow. And every day after that until you do."

I'm tempted. So tempted, I can barely breathe. "What changed from a week ago, when we made our deal?"

"Everything, and nothing. I've never felt that pull toward someone, like I couldn't let you get away. I tried to convince myself it was just phenomenal physical chemistry. But inside, I knew it was more than that. You were like a beacon, the one I didn't realize I needed to find. I thought I was pleasure-cruising through life, but I was actually lost at sea. Until I met you."

"Those are some super-romantic metaphors for a playboy businessman."

"But not for a businessman in love with one woman."

"You said it again," I whisper.

"I'm going to keep saying it. Until you believe it. Until there's no breath left in my body to say it." He cups my face again. "I love you. Take a chance on me. On the us we can be, forever. You won't regret it."

"Are you willing to bet on that?" Just because I'm about

to cave to my deepest romantic desires doesn't mean I can't be sassy. Besides, I know he loves it.

"With everything I have, sweetheart," he says, melting me with one of his irresistible smiles.

"I can't believe I'm doing this…" I lightly beat my fists against the chest that's about to become my favorite pillow. "I'll love you forever, too." I shriek when my feet leave the ground. "But with conditions," I say, holding on for dear life as he spins me around, right there in my tiny hallway.

"Name them."

"So we can negotiate?"

There's a twinkle in his eyes as he shakes his head. "So I can agree to everything and we can seal the deal."

"With a kiss this time?"

"For starters," he says, sealing his lips to mine.

epilogue

HARRISON

THERE ARE A LOT OF "BIG DAYS" on the calendar when you're a businessperson. Valentine's Day is one of the biggest for Eden's business, and she's been burning the midnight oil to get tonight's MatchMakers meetups ready.

Meetups, plural—as in three—because her business has tripled since last year. I'm not claiming responsibility for that increase, but making sure the hottest matchmaker in the city always goes to work with a post-orgasmic smile on her face can't hurt either.

She's still glowing with one of those smiles when she pokes her head through the doorway of our shared home office. "I'm going to check the halls for tonight's events. Do you need anything while I'm out?"

I know she has everything organized, that the checks are unnecessary, but I'd never tell her how to run her business. If she wants to make sure everything's in order—again—then she will. She's meticulous, focused, and driven. We both are, it's one of the many things we have in common.

"I'll go with you," I say, coming around from behind my desk, which now sits across the room from hers.

Neither of us works in here full time, but it's nice to be close to each other when we're putting in extra hours. Proximity to our bed is a perk, too, because watching Eden work is sexy as fuck. Hell, watching her do anything turns me on. A year together and the fire's still blazing as hot as the first time. I know with every cell in my body that's not going to change.

We fucked until we were a sweaty heap an hour ago, yet the second I place my palm on the small of her back, my cock's solid as steel. Her eyes widen and her lips part as she looks up at me. I can't see beneath her buttoned-up blouse, but I'd bet last year's profits her nipples are hard inside whatever sexy bra she's wearing.

I could steer her to our bedroom right now and she'd go. I'm tempted. But that'd put her behind schedule, which would cut into my plan. I'll wait for another taste of my Eden. We have the rest of our lives.

"I know you and Greg have an unveiling coming up," she says, as I grab my keys from the hall table. "Are you sure you have time to gallivant around the city with me?"

"I always have time for you, sweetheart. Especially when there's *gallivanting*." Fuck, I love the way she talks. "Mind if we swing by my office after you check your halls?"

"Of course." One hand on my chest, the other curled around the bulge behind my fly, she leans in and brushes her lips against my jawline. "Whatever you need."

"Hold that thought until we get home."

"Bet on it." She giggles when I smack her perfect ass to

shoo her toward the door. "Aren't you even going to kiss me?"

"Can't. There's never 'just kissing' you. I won't be able to stop once I start."

"I know, and I love it."

"And I love you," I say, wrapping my arms around her after we step onto the elevator. Hard to believe that a year ago, I laughed at the idea of being in love. Now I can't tell her enough.

EDEN

This is my third Valentine's Day as a MatchMakers franchise owner. The first year, I ran the event on my own, and struggled to get twenty people to attend. Last year, I had a folder full of applicants to choose from. Tonight, I have three events. Three! All at premiere locations.

Everything is ready to go. The halls are set up, the decorations impeccable. My employees are more than prepared. There are going to be a lot of happy people tonight. I can't wait to see how many love matches will be made.

Still, I'm glad for the distraction of stopping at Harrison's office. I need to keep busy until it's time for the event. We *could* fill the rest of the day with sex. I could convince him. Easily. But Harrison respects my business, and I do the same. If he has something to take care of, I support him. Always.

A year ago, he waltzed into my event and acted like a

supreme ass. I swore I wouldn't date him if he were the last man alive. Now I can't imagine life without him.

"Where are we going?" I ask, when my handsome, wickedly intelligent boyfriend leads me away from the entrance to his office building, instead of inside.

"Stan's."

I laugh as he tugs me along, as if he can't get to the food truck fast enough. I don't need to ask if he's serious. When it comes to skyscraper burgers, Harrison doesn't joke around.

"There they are, my favorite lovebirds," Stan says, when we come into view. "I know what Harrison wants." That's all he says. He just smiles at me, rather than issuing his usual, *"What can I make for you, Ms. Greene?"* that always follows.

"Ms. Greene."

I turn at Harrison's voice, my bottom lip falling open when he goes down on one knee. "What are you doing?"

"Hoping that's the last time anyone ever calls you Ms. Greene." He takes my hand, looks into my eyes, and opens a velvet box to reveal a glittering, heart-shaped diamond with rubies on each side. "A year ago, I thought love was for suckers. That true, lasting love didn't exist, and love at first sight was just physical attraction. I've never been more wrong in my life, and never happier since. I want to spend my life making you as happy as you've made me. I love you, Eden, with everything I was, am, and will be. Will you marry me?"

"Yes. Oh my God, yes." I cup my free hand over my mouth, then move it higher to wipe the happy tears rolling down my cheek. "I love you so much."

"Best day of my life, with a lifetime of best days still to come," he says, sliding the ring into place. Then he's on his feet, sweeping me off of mine, the way he has since the beginning of our fairytale.

Thank you for reading Dating the Doubter! If you enjoyed this sweet and steamy little instalove romance, I would be so grateful if you would leave a review on Amazon, BookBub, and Goodreads.

xoxo karla

Join Karla's mailing list to stay updated on new releases, sales, freebies, and more!
www.karladoyle.com/newsletter

second epilogue

The Honeymoon

16 months later…

EDEN

WHEN HARRISON OFFERED to take me anywhere in the world for our honeymoon, I told him I didn't care where we went, and I meant it. I just need to be with him.

My friends have spent the last sixteen months guessing Harrison's choice of destination. Greece. Australia. Iceland. Fiji. They couldn't have been further from the truth.

"You're quiet over there." Harrison looks away from the road for a moment to look at me. "Disappointed we're heading to a Lake Erie cottage, instead of boarding an airplane bound for an exotic five-star resort?"

"The opposite. I'm so happy we're honeymooning in Hope Harbor." I reach across the center console and curve my palm over his thigh. "You couldn't have chosen any place better. Thank you for taking me to your grandparents' hometown." The one place he witnessed true love. He's got a pretty deep romantic streak, this husband of mine. Husband. Mine. Two perfect words.

He picks up my hand and brings it to his lips for a kiss. Then smiles and returns his attention to the road.

Countryside gives way to residential neighborhoods as the two-lane highway becomes a small-town street. Within minutes, we're at the top of a gentle hill, bringing the harbor into view. The water ahead is serene and blue, the sky above dotted with puffy white clouds and golden sunshine.

"Look at all the sailboats," I say, craning my neck to take in a marina on my right as we drive over a metal lift-bridge. "Did your grandparents have a boat?"

"No. Wasn't within their budget. We used to sit at the pier and watch them sometimes though. There's a boat parade on Canada Day. It's something to see."

"Oh, we're going miss it by a week. That's too bad."

"We can come back the following weekend."

"Really?"

Stopped at an intersection, he smiles over at me. "Absolutely."

"Won't it be hard to get a rental on a holiday weekend, on such short notice? Or will we just drive down for the day?"

Focused on the bustle of tourist-town traffic, he doesn't answer while making a right-hand turn up a steep hill. Parked cars line both sides of the street, and pedestrians crisscross at a leisurely pace.

I don't need an answer. Knowing Harrison, he started formulating a plan the moment he offered to come back for a second visit. Whatever he decides will be great. It always is.

I lean back in my seat and soak up the scenery. The

hotel on my right looks straight out of a retro photograph. Charming older houses and quaint cottages populate the neighborhood once we reach the top of the hill. Mature, leafy trees shade the sidewalks. It's lovely and peaceful.

Harrison turns left a few blocks up, then makes another left into a driveway, where he shuts off the engine.

"Is this ours?" I ask when he unbuckles his seatbelt.

"It sure is."

"It's adorable." I follow his lead, studying the small bungalow through the windshield while I unbuckle and gather my purse. "I love it already. Thank you for choosing it."

"I didn't choose it," he says, turning to face me, rather than getting out of the car. "My grandparents did."

"Wait—this is your grandparents' house?"

"Was. It went to their kids after they passed. My dad and two aunts. They sold it right away."

"And now it's a rental property." Frequented by many, but cherished by none. I know it has been a decade since he lost his beloved grandparents, but my heart aches for his loss nonetheless. I stroke his handsome face, then cup it in my hand. "We don't have to stay here if it's going to be painful."

"It won't be. I have great memories from the time I spent in this house, and with you, I'm going to make a thousand more."

"A thousand?" I cock my head. "Even our excellent stamina might not be enough to make a thousand memories in two weeks."

"What about during the rest of our lives?" He shifts in place, reaches into his pants pocket to retrieve a single key attached to a heart-shaped fob. "This is our place now, sweetheart. We're not renting it, we own it."

"You bought your grandparents' house?"

He shakes his head. "We bought it. Want to go inside?"

"Oh my God, yes!"

A wide smile crests on his face. He drops a quick kiss on my lips, then he's out of the car, moving around to open the passenger door. Fingers laced with mine, we walk up the short path to the front door.

Key poised to do its duty, I stop at the sight of a carved sign that reads, *The Bernards*, where it's affixed to the exterior wall beside the door. "Was this their sign?"

"It was. Hung exactly in that spot for my lifetime. I took it before the house sold. Never knew why I'd bothered, or why I'd kept it, until I met you."

I throw myself at him, right there on the small stoop. "I love you so much."

"Let's go inside so I can show you much I love you too," he says, trailing his fingertips down my spine until he runs out of bare skin. "How much I need you."

Need. It's our word, and a shiver ripples through me, despite the beautifully warm June day. "How are you going to show me?"

"So many ways, Mrs. Bernard. So many fucking ways." He's behind me as I unlock the door, his hands curled around my hips, his hard cock pressed against my ass.

By the time the door clicks closed behind him, my body is humming. The hotel-room sex we had a few hours ago is a distant memory to my needy body.

"Bathroom?" I whisper as he kisses my neck.

"On the right." He slides his fingers down the front of my dress, over my abdomen, curving them over my mound. "I'll grab our bags from the car. We're going to need them."

I know what that means, and that knowledge sends my pulse into overdrive. My brain is foggy with lust as I move toward the bathroom. It's small but equipped with everything I need—literally. Harrison has been here already, stocking *our* cottage with my favorite products, and duplicates of my hygiene gadgets. He's a planner, my insatiable, sexy husband.

Not only has he provided me with everything I need, he's also left me a gift. I push aside the tissue in the glossy white bag, then remove the contents. A pair of red stilettos, and a note in his unmistakable, strong handwriting.

Wear these. Only these.

Before Harrison, I couldn't imagine being comfortable enough with someone to give up control, to expose all my inner desires and feelings. He makes it easy to be me because he loves every part of me.

I shed the last of my clothing, slide my toes into the glossy red shoes, then step out of the bathroom—naked. Sunlight streams through the living room windows to my right, but I cross the room with my chin up, heading straight for the open bedroom door.

The blinds are closed in here, but candlelight bathes the room. Harrison waits on the bed, propped against a tall, padded headboard. His eyes eat me up as I enter the room, as if it's his first time seeing me naked, though he's seen every inch of me hundreds of times before.

"Fuck me," he says, lazily sliding his fist up and down his thick, hard cock.

"I could...but I'd rather *you* fuck *me*."

"That's exactly what I'm going to do, sweetheart. But not yet. Not until you need me to fuck you so badly, you're begging for my cock."

I'm already there, and he knows it. But I'm a greedy

bride, I want everything else, too. I join him on the bed, edging toward him on my knees until I'm kneeling between his thighs. "Here," I say, gathering my hair in a handheld ponytail.

His nostrils flare as he holds my hair in one fist. He loves this part, and so do I.

Back arched to give him a view of my curves, I lower my head and suck his cock between my lips. Slowly. Until I've taken every thick inch.

He groans as I hollow my cheeks and suck. "Fuck, baby, your mouth feels so good."

The next couple of strokes are mine. Drawn-out releases that end with his crown popping free of my lips, then deliberate, firm descents that only end when my nose brushes his groin. With each upstroke, I swirl my tongue over his tip, lapping the precum like the dessert it is. I love the taste of him. The velvety steel feel of him. The size of him.

And I love it when his fingers curl in my hair.

"Need you to open for me," he says, holding my head and thrusting upward to fill my mouth. "You fucking undo me, Eden."

Jaw slack, I close my eyes as his cock hits the back of my throat. I love undoing him, stealing his control.

"Fuck, I need you." Each thrust is choppier, harder. Deeper. "Always going to need you."

I tighten my lips, sucking hard when he thrusts into my mouth again.

He groans but doesn't give in to my offer. "Not coming down your throat this time," he says, gently pulling me off. In a blink, he's flipped our positions and looks up at me from between my legs. "You're mine now."

My back arches off the bed at the first swipe of his

tongue. God, yes, I'm his. Now and forever.

He eats me as if I'm his last meal. Licking, sucking, flicking. Face buried in my pussy, his growls vibrate against me, through me.

I moan as he slides a finger inside me. Then moan louder when he teases that slick finger into my ass. "More..."

He retreats, then works two fingers inside, flicking my clit faster while finger-fucking my ass.

All I can think about is what's going to happen next—his big cock will be in my ass—and the thought pushes me over. I grab his head, hold him against my pussy as I ride his tongue and fingers through a wave that keeps going and going.

"Fuck, I love when you come," he says, when sensation gets the best of me and I push him away.

I roll onto my stomach and raise my hips. "Fuck me deep." I close my eyes as he fills me in one perfect, swift thrust. Every time is a homecoming. A perfect fit. But right now, I need a different fit.

When he pulls back, I wiggle enough that his cock slips from my pussy. Cheek pressed to the bed, I look over my shoulder at him while grabbing my ass cheeks and spreading them. "I need your cock in my ass."

Even in the dim lighting, the hunger in his eyes is crystal clear. He grabs a bottle of lube from beneath the pillow and spreads it over his shaft, then drizzles some down the valley of my ass.

I want to watch him, but my eyelids flutter closed at the first press of his cock against my rim. This is my favorite part—the hint of burn, the stretch as he breaches my tight hole.

"You're so fucking perfect." Hands gripping my hips, he

pushes deeper. Slowly, but unrelenting. "Going to bury every inch of my dick in your sexy ass."

I bite my lip as he gives me more, more. There's so much, and I want it all. "I need to come."

"Under the pillow, baby."

I slip my hand under and find my vibrator, then position it against my clit as his hips press against my backside.

He moans when the vibe whirs to life. "That feels too good. I need to fuck you so, so deep."

"Do it." The spiral is already building between my legs. "Fuck me deep."

One hand on the small of my back, he pulls out, then fills me again, burying himself to the balls in my ass. Then again. Again.

Every nerve ending is awake and on fire as he fills my ass with his steel-hard dick. I'm on the edge, trying to hold off, but it's too good. "I'm coming..." I pant the words out before losing all control, riding the vibrator while he fucks my ass like a rutting beast.

My rutting beast. The man who makes all my dreams come true, including the filthy ones I never thought I'd share, let alone experience.

"Memory number one, only nine-hundred-and-ninety-nine to go," I say, once he's lying beside me, one arm and leg slung possessively over my body.

His chuckle rumbles against my neck as he pulls me closer. "And then we'll make more."

"Deal." I tip my head up and smile at him. My husband. My sexy beast. My best friend. My happily ever after.

also by karla doyle

12 Days (Hope Harbor)

Shifting Gears (Under the Hood #1)

Dad Bod Wingman (Hope Harbor)

Cup of Sugar (Close to Home #1)

Icing on the Cake (Close to Home #2)

Sweet as Candy (Close to Home #3)

Close to Home Box Set (Books 1—3)

Gift Wrapped

Wedded Miss

Dating the Doubter

Fleshing It Out (Hope Harbor)

Body of Work (Very Personal Training #1)

Worth the Wait (Very Personal Training #2)

Very Personal Training Box Set (Books 1 & 2)

More Than Words

Crossing the Line

Game Plan

Stealing Home

Visit Karla's website for the most up-to-date list.

www.karladoyle.com

about the author

 A small-town girl with some big-city experience, Karla resides in Southwestern Ontario with her husband and two children. She studied fashion design in college and spent 20+ years working in that industry before succumbing to the writing muse. When she's not writing the sexy stories that swirl around in her head, you can find her cuddled up with a book and her adorable pets.

Karla loves hearing from readers! Connect with her online, or send her an email: karla@karladoyle.com.

Join Karla's mailing list to stay up to date on all her news.
www.karladoyle.com/newsletter